I dedicate this book to my parents, Drs. Ronald and Betty Crutcher for showing me unconditional love and providing me a life beyond my wildest dreams.

www.mascotbooks.com

Heart Picked: Elizabeth's Adoption Tale

Second Edition

For more information, please contact:
Mascot Books
560 Herndon Parkway #120
Herndon, VA 20170
info@mascotbooks.com

CPSIA Code: PRT1115B
ISBN: 978-1-63177-090-6

Printed in the United States

HEART PICKED

ELIZABETH'S ADOPTION TALE

written by
Sara Crutcher

To Mel + Ramsey,
You were heart
picked!
continue to
spread love!
XO Sara Crutcher

One sunny morning, Elizabeth's parents are waiting in the kitchen to eat breakfast together as a family like they do every morning.

Elizabeth's dad calls upstairs to see if she is ready for school.

Elizabeth comes down dressed in one of her fancy, blue dresses and a big hat. Her mom asks, "Elizabeth sweetie, what are you wearing? Is everything okay? You usually don't play dress-up before school."

Elizabeth looks down at the floor and explains, "I'm nervous for Daddy to come to my school today for family week. What if the other kids say we don't look alike?"

Elizabeth's mom says with a comforting smile, "We don't have to look alike to love each other. You were heart picked! Always remember that we love you very much and it's okay that the three of us don't look exactly alike. We're not twins, silly. Now, please put on your clothes for school."

Once dressed and downstairs, Elizabeth perks up seeing her favorite fruit on the table.

Her dad cheerfully says, "I'm excited to have lunch with you today for family week. Don't forget to save me a seat!"

At school, Elizabeth's classmates share family stories and meet all of the parents who came for family week. Elizabeth sees her friend Holly standing with her dad. They look a lot alike which makes Elizabeth nervous all over again.

"Hey, Elizabeth. This is my dad," says Holly.

"Hi, Holly's dad. My name is Elizabeth!"

Elizabeth looks up and sees her dad walking in.
Holly looks confused and asks, "That's your dad?
You don't look like him."

FAMILY WEEK!

Elizabeth remembers what her mom told her earlier that morning and announces, "Not all families have to look alike to love each other."

After school, Elizabeth is anxious to tell her mom about her day. "Mommy, Holly said I didn't look like Daddy at school today and it made me nervous for a second. Then I told her what you said and I felt much better!"

Her mom replies, "That's right, sweetie. We adopted you to add more love to our family. Always remember we love you very much, and it's okay that the three of us don't look exactly alike. You were heart picked with love! You didn't grow under my heart, but in it!"

"What's adoption again, Mommy?"
Elizabeth asks.

Elizabeth's mom starts telling a familiar story. "When you were born, your birth mommy and daddy loved you very much. They wanted you to have everything you needed to grow big and strong, eat healthy foods, and have a loving place to play and learn. They were not able to give that to you. Your dad and I were able to give you all those things and more, so we adopted you and became a family."

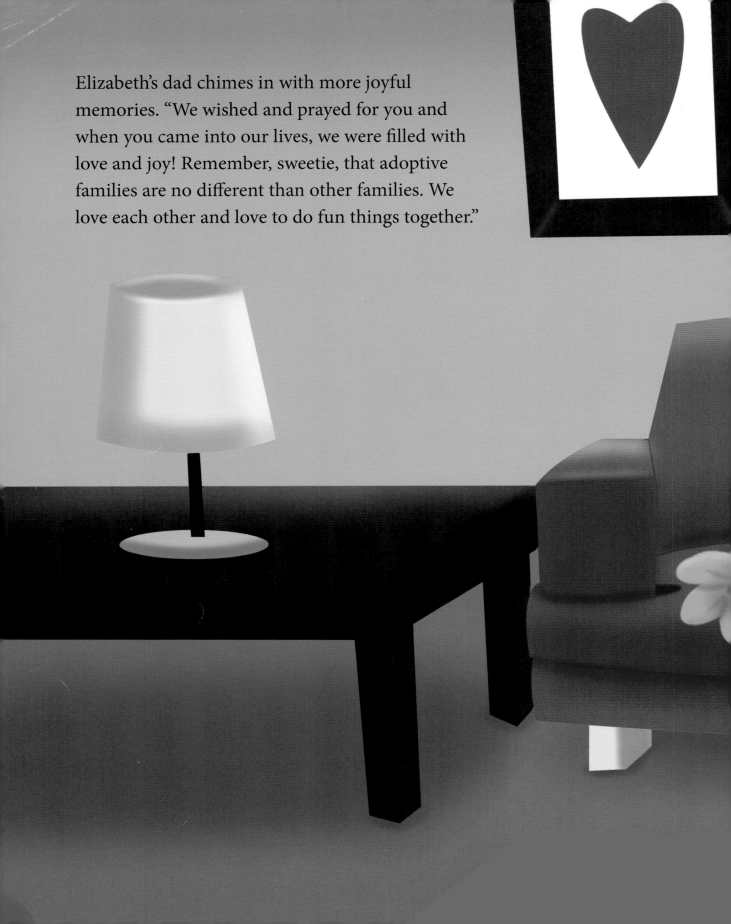

Elizabeth's dad chimes in with more joyful memories. "We wished and prayed for you and when you came into our lives, we were filled with love and joy! Remember, sweetie, that adoptive families are no different than other families. We love each other and love to do fun things together."

"We love to go to the zoo…

…and play in the park."

"We ride bikes and…

...play our instruments."

"We would not be able to do those fun things without you!" adds Elizabeth's mom.

Elizabeth is so excited to have such an amazing family. "I am so happy you heart picked me!!! I love you!" shouts Elizabeth. "Mom, I can't wait for you to come to my school and meet all of my friends too!"

"Now, who wants ice cream?"
Elizabeth's mom asks.

"I DO!" Elizabeth beams.

ABOUT THE AUTHOR

First-time author Sara Elizabeth Neal Crutcher is behind this touching and personal narrative that affirms love is what truly makes a family.

Sara believes her greatest blessing came at just six weeks old in Greensboro, North Carolina when she was adopted into a loving and supportive family. At five years old, Sara recalls her parents sitting her down to explain her adoption. Although at the time she did not fully understand what adoption meant, she was reassured that she was heart picked and surrounded by unconditional love. Sara wrote *Heart Picked: Elizabeth's Adoption Tale* to share a glimpse of her journey and also to support adopted children and the families who love them.

Sara Elizabeth Neal Crutcher is an advertising executive, entrepreneur and blogger. She graduated from Hampton University with a degree in advertising. She enjoys spending time with her family and friends, traveling, reading novels, and playing her violin.